The Babies on the Bus

Karen Katz

Henry Holt and Company New York

The wheels on the bus go **round and round,** all through the town.

The doors on the bus

open and close,
open and close,
open and close.

The doors on the bus

open
and
close,

all through the town.

The driver on the bus says,

"Move on back,
move on back,
move on back!"

The driver on the bus says,

"Move
on
back!"

all through the town.

The babies on the bus sing,

"LA-LA-LA!
LA-LA-LA!
LA-LA-LA!"

The babies on the bus sing,

"LA-LA-LA!"

all through the town.

The wipers on the bus go

swish, swish, swish!
Swish, swish, swish,
Swish, swish, swish!

The wipers on the bus go

swish, swish,
swish,

all through the town.

The babies on the bus bounce

bumpity bump, bumpity bump, bumpity bump!

The babies on the bus bounce

bumpity bump,

all through the town.

The horn on the bus goes **toot, toot, toot,** all through the town.

The babies on the bus cry,
"Waah! Waah! Waah!"
all through the town.

The driver on the bus says,

"Shush, shush, shush.
Shush, shush, shush.
Shush, shush, shush."

The driver on the bus says,
"shush, shush, shush,"
all through the town.

The babies on
the bus fall

fast asleep,
fast asleep,
fast asleep.

The babies on
the bus fall

fast
asleep,

all through
the town.

The motor on the bus goes

zoom, zoom, zoom!
zoom, zoom, zoom!
zoom, zoom, zoom!

The motor on the bus goes

zoom, zoom, zoom,

all through the town.

The driver on the bus says,

"Everyone up! Everyone up! Everyone up!"

The driver on the bus says,

"Everyone UP!"

all through the town.

The babies on the bus say,
"Bye-bye, bus! Bye-bye, bus!

Bye-bye, bus!"

The babies on the bus say,

"Bye-bye, bus!"

Now it's time to go.

EXIT

**For Lena and Gary
and all the bouncing
babies everywhere**

Henry Holt and Company, LLC, *Publishers since 1866*
175 Fifth Avenue, New York, New York 10010
mackids.com

Henry Holt® is a registered trademark of Henry Holt and Company, LLC.
Copyright © 2011 by Karen Katz
All rights reserved.

Library of Congress Cataloging-in-Publication Data
Katz, Karen.
Babies on the bus / by Karen Katz. — 1st ed.
p.   cm.
Summary: Presents lyrics to the well-known song, interspersed with additional verses about babies.
ISBN 978-0-8050-9011-6
1. Children's songs, English—United States—Texts. [1. Folk songs. 2. Songs. 3. Buses—Songs and music.] I. Title.
PZ8.3.K1283Bab 2011   782.42—dc22   [E]   2010039229

First Edition—2011 / Book designed by April Ward
Printed in March 2011 in China by South China Printing Company Ltd.,
Dongguan City, Guangdong Province

1 3 5 7 9 10 8 6 4 2